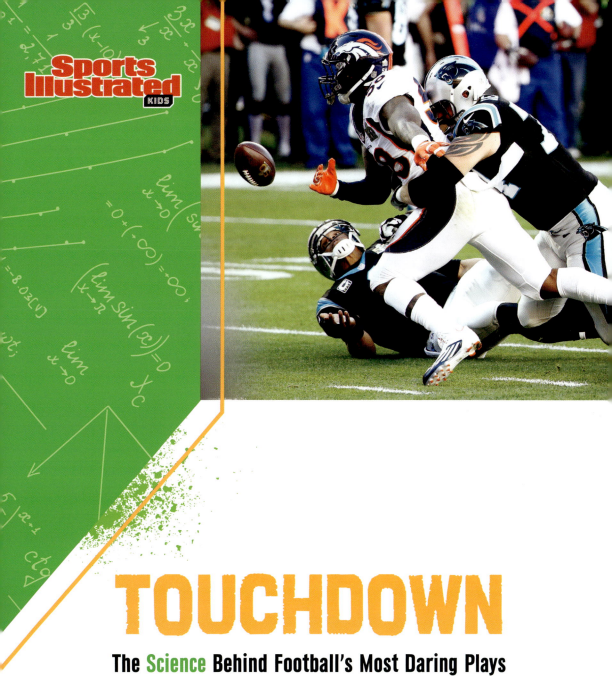

Sports Illustrated KIDS

TOUCHDOWN

The Science Behind Football's Most Daring Plays

by Allan Morey

CAPSTONE PRESS
a capstone imprint

Published by Capstone Press, an imprint of Capstone
1710 Roe Crest Drive, North Mankato, Minnesota 56003
capstonepub.com

Copyright © 2025 by Capstone. All rights reserved. No part of
this publication may be reproduced in whole or in part, or stored
in a retrieval system, or transmitted in any form or by any means,
electronic, mechanical, photocopying, recording, or otherwise,
without written permission of the publisher.

SPORTS ILLUSTRATED KIDS is a trademark of ABG-SI LLC.
Used with permission.

Library of Congress Cataloging-in-Publication Data
Names: Morey, Allan, author. Title: Touchdown : the science behind
football's most daring plays / by Allan Morey.
Description: North Mankato, Minnesota: Capstone Press, 2025.
Series: Sports illustrated kids. Science behind the plays | Includes bibliographical
references and index.
Audience: Ages 8–11 | Audience: Grades 4–6
Summary: "Franco Harris's immaculate reception in 1972. Marcus Allen's run to
glory in Super Bowl 1984. Tom Dempsey's 63-yard game-winning field goal in
1970. Von Miller's notorious sacks in game after game. Every aspect of football
showcases science, from throwing to hitting to running to catching. Momentum,
velocity, force, and more are on full display in these game-changing football
plays"—Provided by publisher.
Identifiers: LCCN 2024032139 (print) | LCCN 2024032140 (ebook) | ISBN
9781669091912 (hardcover) | ISBN 9781669092131 (paperback) | ISBN
9781669091950 (pdf) | ISBN 9781669092148 (epub) | ISBN 9781669092155
(kindle edition) Subjects: LCSH: Football—Juvenile literature. | Sports
sciences—Juvenile literature.
Classification: LCC GV950.7 .M67 2025 (print) | LCC GV950.7 (ebook) | DDC
796.332—dc23/eng/20240821
LC record available at https://lccn.loc.gov/2024032139
LC ebook record available at https://lccn.loc.gov/2024032140

Editorial Credits
Editor: Christianne Jones; Designer: Jaime Willems; Media Researcher:
Svetlana Zhurkin; Production Specialist: Whitney Shaefer

Image Credits
Associated Press: cover (left), 8, Al Messerschmidt, 23, File, 13, 15, File/Harry
Cabluck, 28, Hall of Fame, 27, JTR, 12, Kevin Terrell, 25, Peter Read Miller,
cover (right), 19; Capstone: Jaime Willems, 16 (left); Getty Images: Al Bello, 1,
11, Bettmann, 17, Ezra Shaw, 29, Focus on Sport, 9, 20, 22, George Gojkovich,
26, GeorgiosArt, 10 (Newton), Justin Edmonds, 7, Rob Brown, 21; Shutterstock:
Deviney Designs (powder), cover and throughout, Eugene Onischenko,
5, lumyai l sweet, 10 (referee), Marina Sun (math background), cover and
throughout, Vector Tradition (football), back cover and throughout

Any additional websites and resources referenced in this book are not
maintained, authorized, or sponsored by Capstone. All product and company
names are trademarks™ or registered® trademarks of their respective holders.

Printed and bound in the USA. PO 6121

TABLE OF CONTENTS

Science and Football 4

Chapter One
Sack Attack 6

Chapter Two
Game-Winning Field Goal 12

Chapter Three
Breakout Run 18

Chapter Four
Immaculate Reception 24

Glossary 30
Read More 31
Internet Sites 31
Index 32
About the Author 32

Words in **BOLD** are in the glossary.

SCIENCE AND FOOTBALL

A typical NFL game is four 15-minute quarters. That means 60 minutes of hard-hitting action. The offense and defense are battling every second. In those 60 minutes, the game averages 150 plays. That's 150 chances for players to show off their skills.

But no matter how talented the players are, science is the biggest star. It plays a key role in all the action. The ball needs to be thrown at the right angle and **velocity** to hit its target. And players use **force**, **energy**, and **leverage** to move the ball downfield.

Let's explore how science affected some of the most memorable plays in football history.

DEFINITIONS

leverage: the force needed to lift and/or move objects

velocity: the speed and direction of a moving object

force: an action that changes or maintains the motion of a body or object

energy: force that causes things to move

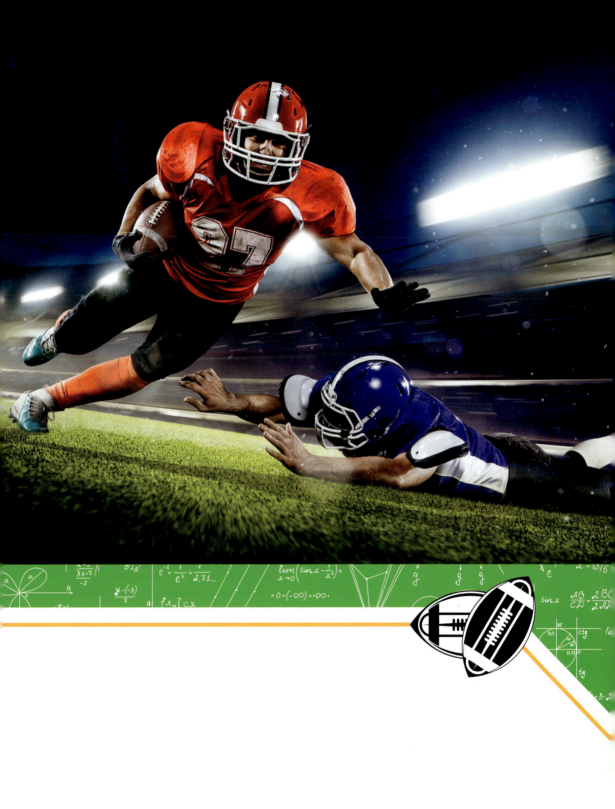

CHAPTER ONE

SACK ATTACK

One of the most disruptive defensive plays is the quarterback sack. A defender bursts through the offensive line. He tackles the quarterback before he can get rid of the ball. This causes the offense to lose yards. It can also change the outcome of the game.

Linebacker Von Miller was a sack master. He started his career with the Denver Broncos. On February 7, 2016, they faced the Carolina Panthers in Super Bowl 50. The Panthers had racked up an impressive 15–1 record that year. They were favorites to beat the Broncos. But Miller had other plans.

Von Miller sacked quarterback Ryan Fitzpatrick during a game in Denver.

FACT

Quarterback sacks were not counted as an official NFL statistic until 1982.

Around eight minutes into the game, the Broncos had the Panthers pinned deep in their own territory. As Miller lined up for the next play, he was full of **potential energy**. That energy was stored in his muscles. It would propel him forward with great force and **speed**.

Just as the ball was hiked to Panthers quarterback Cam Newton, Miller took off. All of Miller's potential energy turned into **kinetic energy**, which is the energy in a moving object. Or in this case, the energy in a linebacker barreling down on the QB.

SECRETARY OF DEFENSE

David "Deacon" Jones was a powerhouse on defense. He even helped coin the term "sack." He said, "You take all the offensive linemen and put them in a burlap bag . . . You're sacking them . . . And that's what you're doing with a quarterback." Nobody knows how many sacks Jones had during his career. He played before they were counted as an official stat.

An offensive lineman moved to block Miller. Miller jerked right to fake him out. Then Miller planted his right foot on the turf. The spikes on his cleats dug into the turf, providing **friction**. This force kept his foot from slipping as he turned sharply to dart around the offensive lineman.

Miller used kinetic energy and friction to move around the lineman.

DEFINITIONS

potential energy: stored energy

kinetic energy: the energy of motion

friction: a force that slows down or stops motion between two things that are in contact

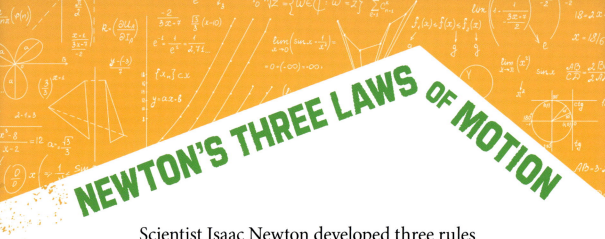

NEWTON'S THREE LAWS OF MOTION

Scientist Isaac Newton developed three rules about motion. These are known as Newton's laws of motion, and they play a huge role in every game.

1. An object remains at rest or in motion until it's affected by a force.
2. The greater the mass of an object, the more force it will take to move it. In other words, force equals mass times acceleration ($F = ma$).
3. For every action, there is an equal and opposite reaction.

What happened next is a perfect example of the first law of motion. This law states that an object remains at rest or in motion until it's affected by a force. A quarterback standing in the pocket is at rest until a defender slams into him by force.

Miller rushed forward and smacked Cam Newton. That force sent Newton sprawling backward. He lost his grip on the ball. Fumble! The ball bounced into the end zone. Broncos defender Malik Jackson dove onto it for the recovery. Touchdown! The Broncos went on to win the game.

The force from Miller's sack caused a fumble.

CHAPTER TWO

GAME-WINNING FIELD GOAL

Being a kicker is a high-pressure job. A last-second field goal can be the difference between a stunning victory or a crushing defeat. Kicker Tom Dempsey found himself in that position on November 8, 1970, when his New Orleans Saints faced the Detroit Lions.

Detroit Lions running back Mel Farr hopped over a Saints defender on his way to score a touchdown.

The Lions were one of the league's best teams that season. With just two seconds left in the game, the Saints were down 17–16. They had the ball and one chance to win. But there was a problem. Dempsey would have to kick a record 63-yard field goal. That was seven yards longer than the record at the time.

FACT

Tom Dempsey was born without fingers on his right hand and without toes on his right foot, which was his kicking foot. He used a special shoe with a flat kicking surface on the front.

Field goals may look easy, but there are several steps and lots of science involved. First, the center applies force to the ball as he hikes it to the holder. The holder uses the friction of his hands against the leather to catch and hold the ball. Then in one fluid motion, he brings the ball point down to the ground with its laces facing forward.

Next, the kicker rushes forward, turning potential energy into kinetic energy. He plants one foot as the friction of his cleats on the turf hold it in place. Using the **momentum** of his body and motion of his hips, he whips his other foot forward in an arc. As his leg **accelerates**, its kinetic energy increases. As his foot connects with the ball, all that energy is transferred to it. That energy launches the ball into the air.

DEFINITIONS

accelerates: increases speed

momentum: the force or speed created by movement

FACT
About 25 percent of NFL points are from field goals.

Dempsey planted his left foot and used momentum to swing his right leg forward.

Lastly, the ball has a battle with wind **resistance** and **gravity**. Also known as drag, wind resistance is the force that pushes against the surface of the football as it sails through the air. Gravity is the force pulling the ball back down to the ground. If Dempsey didn't kick the football with enough velocity, wind resistance would slow it down. The ball wouldn't reach the goal post before gravity pulled it down, and the field goal would fail.

The angle the ball is kicked also affects how far it will fly. Too high an angle, and wind resistance has more time to slow down the ball. Too low an angle, and a defender might reach up and block the kick.

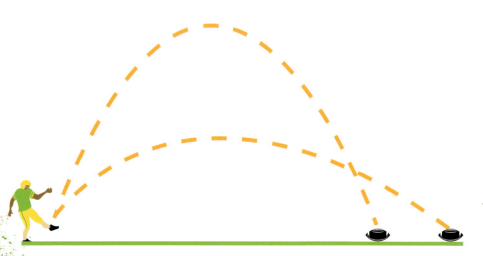

THE ANGLE OF THE KICK DETERMINES HOW FAR THE BALL WILL TRAVEL.

gravity: an invisible force that pulls objects toward each other; Earth's gravity pulls objects toward the ground

resistance: an opposing or slowing force

DEFINITIONS

Dempsey applied the perfect amount of force to send the ball over the crossbar.

That day, science was working for Dempsey. He applied just enough force to get the ball over the crossbar. The kick was up and good! The Saints won because of Dempsey's last-second heroics.

FACT

Typically, the best angle to kick the ball is about 45 degrees.

CHAPTER THREE

BREAKOUT RUN

A breakout run is electric. And if that breakout run happens during a Super Bowl game, it's even more shocking. On January 22, 1984, running back Marcus Allen proved that to be true. His Los Angeles Raiders had the lead against Washington in Super Bowl XVIII.

With 12 seconds left in the third quarter, the Raiders had the ball on their own 26-yard line. As soon as the ball was hiked to quarterback Jim Plunkett, Allen turned his potential energy into kinetic energy.

Marcus Allen cut back on a run, tricking the defense.

Allen rushed to the left and received the handoff from Plunkett. As Allen turned to cut upfield, two defenders stood in his way. Could he get past them? He could if he relied on Newton's second law of motion. That's exactly what he did.

Offensive linemen held off defenders while Allen secured the handoff from Plunkett.

Allen used friction, acceleration, and kinetic energy to outrun the defense.

Allen planted his feet. The friction of his cleats digging into the turf stopped him. A running back's acceleration depends on his mass and the amount of force he applies. At slightly more than 200 pounds, Allen didn't have a lot of mass to move. And he was a powerful runner with a lot of potential energy in his leg muscles. He quickly changed direction and accelerated.

A defender went to grab Allen, but he didn't have enough friction in his grip. Allen slipped through his grasp, cutting upfield.

Leverage is the force needed to move an object. And leverage is what the Raiders' offensive linemen used on Washington's defenders to get them out of Allen's way. Thanks to the linemen, there was a huge hole in the defense for Allen to run through.

Allen slips through a defender's grip, cutting back upfield.

speed: how fast an object changes position

DEFINITIONS

Allen broke tackles and outran defenders multiple times during the Super Bowl.

With no one blocking his path, Allen picked up speed. Speed is the result of potential energy transferring to kinetic energy. The more energy Allen had, the greater his speed. Nobody could catch him. Allen ran 74 yards for a touchdown! That remarkable play sealed the win for the Raiders. It's considered one of the best runs in NFL history.

SUPER RUSHING STATS

Longest Running Play—99 yards, Derrick Henry, Tennessee Titans (2018) and Tony Dorsett, Dallas Cowboys (1982)

Most Rushing Yards in a Game—296 yards, Adrian Peterson, Minnesota Vikings (2007)

Most Rushing Yards in a Season—2,105 yards, Eric Dickerson, Los Angeles Rams (1984)

Most Rushing Yards in a Career—18,355 yards, Emmitt Smith, Dallas Cowboys (1990–2002), Arizona Cardinals (2003–04)

CHAPTER FOUR

IMMACULATE RECEPTION

Some football plays are impressive. Others are record-breaking. Then there are the ones that are almost too remarkable to believe, such as the "Immaculate Reception." This play happened on December 23, 1972. The Pittsburgh Steelers were facing the Oakland Raiders in the AFC playoffs.

With 22 seconds left in the game, the Steelers were down 7–6. They had the ball on their 40-yard line. It was fourth down, with 10 yards needed to get a first down. Things seemed hopeless. The Steelers needed a big play to stay in the game. What they got was a miracle of science.

The Steelers' center hiked the ball to quarterback Terry Bradshaw. Bradshaw stepped back to pass. He scrambled away from a defender. Then he launched the ball to running back John Fuqua.

Bradshaw planted his left foot as he pulled back to throw.

Throwing a football is not easy. It needs to be thrown with a pointy end going forward. That helps it cut through the air. Otherwise, it would lose the battle with wind resistance. Drag would push it off course, causing an inaccurate pass.

When Bradshaw released the football, his index finger applied force to the football's laces. This force caused the football to spiral. A spiral motion helps lower the drag on the ball, which leads to a more accurate pass.

Bradshaw's pass hit a defender's helmet and bounced back in the air.

Bradshaw's pass was on target. But as Fuqua reached up to snag the pass, Raiders safety Jack Tatum rushed forward to block the pass. Instead, the ball hit Tatum's helmet. As Newton's third law of motion states, there is an equal and opposite reaction for every action. The force from the helmet pushing back on the ball caused the ball to bounce up in the air.

FACT

What shape is a football? It's technically a prolate spheroid. That's a fancy way of saying it is longer than it is wide.

27

Franco Harris grabbed the ball out of the air and sprinted toward the end zone.

For a moment, the players on the field stood still. They thought the play had ended with an incomplete pass. But Steelers running back Franco Harris saw the ball bounce off Tatum's helmet, and he didn't stop moving.

Harris snagged the ball out of the air. With his built-up speed, Harris rumbled down field into the end zone. Touchdown and a Steelers victory!

From the opening kickoff to the last whistle, science is a part of every football game. Every kick. Every throw. Every snap. Science is behind every single play. And when you mix science with incredible athletes, you will rarely be disappointed.

Patrick Mahomes throws a pass during Super Bowl LVIII, showcasing a perfect mix of science and athletic ability.

GLOSSARY

accelerate (ak-SEH-luh-rayt)—to increase speed

energy (EH-nuhr-jee)—the ability to do work

force (FOHRS)—an action that changes or maintains the motion of a body or object

friction (FRIK-shuhn)—a force that slows down or stops motion between two things that are in contact

gravity (GRAH-vuh-tee)—an invisible force that pulls objects toward each other; Earth's gravity pulls objects toward the ground

kinetic energy (kuh-NEH-tik EH-nuhr-jee)—the energy of motion

leverage (LEH-vuh-rij)—the force needed to lift and/or move objects

momentum (moh-MEN-tuhm)—the force or speed created by movement

potential energy (puh-TEN-shuhl EH-nuhr-jee)—stored energy

resistance (rih-ZIH-stuhns)—an opposing or slowing force

speed (SPEED)—how fast an object changes position

velocity (vuh-LAH-suh-tee)—the speed and direction of a moving object

READ MORE

Harris, Beatrice. *STEM in Football*. Buffalo, NY: Cavendish Square Publishing, 2025.

James, India. *Football*. New York: Crabtree Publishing, 2025.

McCollum, Sean. *Full STEAM Football: Science, Technology, Engineering, Arts, and Mathematics of the Game*. North Mankato, MN: Capstone Publishing, 2019.

INTERNET SITES

How Stuff Works: Football
entertainment.howstuffworks.com/physics-of-football.htm

U.S. National Science Foundation: Science of NFL
nsf.gov/news/special_reports/football/index.jsp

Ward's World: Put Your Spin on Football Science
wardsworld.wardsci.com/home/put-your-spin-on-football-science

INDEX

accelerate, 10, 14, 21
Allen, Marcus, 18–23

Bradshaw, Terry, 25–27

Dempsey, Tom, 12–13, 15–17

friction, 9, 14, 21–22
fumble, 11
Fuqua, John, 25, 27

gravity, 16, 26, 28

Harris, Franco, 28

Jones, David "Deacon", 8

kinetic energy, 8, 9, 14, 18, 21, 23

leverage, 4, 22

Mahomes, Patrick, 29
mass, 10, 21
Miller, Von, 6–9, 11
momentum, 14, 15

Newton, Isaac, 10
Newton's laws of motion, 10–11, 20, 27

potential energy, 8–9, 14, 18, 21, 23

resistance, 16, 26

sacks, 6–8, 11
speed, 8, 14, 22–23, 28
spiral, 26

Tatum, Jack, 27

velocity, 4, 16

ABOUT THE AUTHOR

Some of Allan Morey's favorite childhood memories are from the time he spent on a farm in Wisconsin. Every day he saw cows, chickens, and sheep. He even had a pet pig named Pete. He developed a great appreciation of animals, big and small. Allan currently lives in St. Paul, Minnesota, with his family and dogs, Stitch and Enzo, who keep him company while he writes children's books.